Disney

SnowWhite
and the Seven Dwarfs

Ladybird

Once upon a time there lived a beautiful young princess named Snow White. Her father was dead, and her stepmother the Queen hated Snow White. She was jealous of her beauty and forced her to dress in rags and work in the castle.

The Queen had a magic mirror that she spoke to every day. "Magic mirror on the wall," she would say, "who is the fairest of them all?" The mirror always told the Queen she was the fairest. But one day, it replied:

Famed is thy beauty, Majesty,
But hold – a lovely maid I see –
Alas, she is more fair than thee…
Lips red as a rose, hair black
*   as ebony, skin white as snow…*

"Snow White!" hissed the angry Queen.

As the Queen looked in her mirror, Snow White was getting water from the well, singing while she worked. Her voice was so lovely that a prince who was passing by stopped to listen.

Snow White was startled and ran away when she saw the Prince, but he was so kind and handsome that she came out onto the castle balcony. As they gazed at each other they knew they were falling in love.

The Queen, glancing out of her window, saw the Prince and Snow White. She grew wild with jealousy. "I must destroy her!" she said to herself, and she summoned her chief huntsman.

The huntsman knelt before the Queen.

"Take Snow White deep into the forest and kill her," she commanded him. "To prove that you have done the deed, bring me her heart in this box."

The huntsman was shocked. But he had to obey his Queen.

"Yes, your Majesty," he said quietly.

The huntsman took Snow White into the forest as the Queen had ordered. But he could not bring himself to kill the lovely Princess.

"Run away, child," he told her, "and never go back to the castle!" He put the heart of a dead animal in the box to take back to the Queen.

Alone in the forest, Snow White was frightened. But the birds and animals gathered round to comfort her. And the next day they led her to a cosy little cottage.

There were seven tiny chairs in the cottage, so Snow White thought seven small children must live there. When she looked around, she saw that everything was very untidy. "These children must be orphans," she said to herself, "with no one to look after them. Perhaps if I tidy up, they'll let me stay."

Snow White began to dust and sweep, and all her forest friends helped her.

Not far away, the people who lived in the cottage were on their way home from work. They were not children, but seven dwarfs who worked in a mine.

"Heigh-ho, heigh-ho, it's home from work we go!" they sang as they marched along. But they stopped singing when they saw the light on in their cottage.

"Something's in there!" they exclaimed.

Inside the cottage, Snow White had gone upstairs and fallen fast asleep across the seven little beds she'd found. The animals had covered her up, then scampered back into the forest.

The dwarfs crept into the cottage, scared they might find a robber or a goblin inside.

Instead, they found soup bubbling in a pot on the fire.

"Something's cooking!" said the dwarf called Happy. "And it smells good!"

But the other dwarfs were still worried about who might be in their house. They decided to go upstairs to investigate.

They found Snow White asleep in their bedroom. "It's a girl!" said the dwarf called Doc.

Just then Snow White woke up and saw the dwarfs. She was as surprised as they were. "You're not children at all," she said. "You're little men!"

Snow White had read the names on the little beds, so she knew that the dwarfs were called Happy, Sneezy, Sleepy, Dopey, Bashful, Doc and Grumpy. She told them what had happened to her, and how she had come to their cottage.

"If I go back, the Queen will kill me," she said. "Please let me stay here."

The dwarfs were happy to let Snow White stay with them, especially when they remembered the delicious-smelling soup simmering on the fire.

"Time for supper!" they said, rushing downstairs.

"Just a minute," said Snow White.
"You'll have to wash first!"

The dwarfs tried to convince Snow White that they didn't need a wash, but she wasn't fooled. To please her, they marched out to the tub in the garden and gave their hands and faces a good scrubbing.

Only Grumpy stubbornly refused to go. "You're all a bunch of old nanny goats!" he said sourly to the other dwarfs.

The dwarfs looked at Grumpy. Then they looked at each other and nodded. "Get 'im, men!" said Doc.

Before he knew what was happening, Grumpy had been picked up and dumped in the tub. As he fumed and fussed, the dwarfs washed him till he shone.

Meanwhile, in the castle, the Queen learned from her mirror that Snow White was still alive and living with the seven dwarfs.

Furious that she had been deceived, the Queen vowed to kill Snow White with her own hands and went quickly to the deepest dungeon in the palace. There she worked spells of witchcraft and black magic.

She mixed a potion that would turn her into an old pedlar woman. In this disguise, she would visit Snow White – and destroy her.

That night, the dwarfs' cottage was alive with merriment. After supper, the dwarfs got out their musical instruments and played one lively tune after another. Snow White danced with each of the dwarfs, and sang along to the music.

At last it was bedtime. The dwarfs settled themselves downstairs so that Snow White could have their beds. Upstairs, Snow White knelt beside one of the beds and clasped her hands. "Bless the seven little men who have been so kind to me," she prayed. Then she lay down and fell into a deep, contented sleep.

In her secret chamber the Queen, now transformed into a toothless old hag, was busy making a deadly present for Snow White. She dipped a bright red apple into a vat of poison, then chanted a magic spell over it.

"One bite of this," she hissed, "and Snow White will fall into the sleeping death! Only love's first kiss will be able to revive her – and there's no chance of that! The dwarfs will think she's dead and bury her alive! Hah!"

As she put the apple in a basket the witch screeched over and over, "Buried alive! Buried alive!" Then, carrying the basket under her arm, she got into a small boat and set off for the dwarfs' cottage.

Her bulging eyes shone wickedly in the pale moonlight, and an evil grin spread across her face as she thought of the cruel fate that awaited Snow White.

Next morning, as the dwarfs left for their work in the mine, Doc said to Snow White, "Remember, don't let *anyone* in the house! That kwicked ween – I mean, wicked Queen – is full of witchcraft, and she might just trick you!"

"I'll be careful," Snow White promised, giving Doc a goodbye kiss.

Snow White kissed each one of the dwarfs as they left. Grumpy was the last to leave. "Now I'm warnin' ya," he said gruffly, "don't let nobody or nothin' in the house!"

"Oh, Grumpy, you *do* like me!" Snow White exclaimed happily, and she planted a big kiss on his forehead.

Grumpy smiled adoringly, then quickly remembered himself. "Aw, stop that mushy stuff," he said, scowling again as he rushed off to join the others.

When the dwarfs had gone, Snow White went inside to begin preparing their evening meal. As a special treat, she decided to bake them some gooseberry pies.

She was just putting the finishing touches to the last one when a voice said, "Making pies, dearie?"

Startled, Snow White looked up and saw an old woman at the window. "Why, yes," she replied. "Gooseberry pies." She remembered her promise to the dwarfs, but what harm could there be in talking to a poor old woman?

"It's apple pies the menfolk like," the old woman said. "Pies made with apples like this!" And she took the poisoned apple from her basket.

"It does look delicious," said Snow White, reaching out for it.

Snow White's animal friends had been fretting and scurrying about anxiously ever since the disguised Queen arrived. They knew she meant to harm Snow White. Now, just as Snow White was about to take the apple, a flock of birds swooped down and knocked it out of the old woman's hand. Then they began pecking at the old woman and flapping their wings in her face.

"Go away! Leave me alone!" cried the old woman, trying to fight them off.

"Oh, stop it!" said Snow White, rushing outside and shooing the birds away. The birds fluttered helplessly back to their tree as the pedlar picked up the apple.

Snow White took the old woman inside and helped her to a chair. The animals rushed to the window to watch. When Snow White went to get the old woman a drink of water, the woman gave the animals an evil look. Frightened, they ran away to get the dwarfs.

"Something must be – ah-choo! – wrong," cried Sneezy, when the animals began pushing and tugging them towards the cottage.

"Maybe the Queen's got Snow White!" said Sleepy.

"The Queen!" cried Doc. "Let's go!" And they raced home.

But the dwarfs were not fast enough. At the cottage, the wicked old woman was holding the juicy red apple out to Snow White. "This is a magic wishing apple," she told her. "It will give you anything your heart desires. Go on, take it!"

Snow White thought at once of the Prince she had met in the castle garden. Taking the apple, she said, "I wish that I will meet my Prince again, and that together we will travel to his kingdom." Then she took a bite.

"Oh! I feel so strange," said Snow White. And with a soft moan, she fell to the floor.

"It is done!" shrieked the old woman. "Now I'll be the fairest in the land!" She cackled triumphantly as she ran from the cottage.

Outside a sudden clap of thunder shook the sky. Lightning ripped through the clouds, and rain tumbled down. The Queen hurried through the woods, eager to return to her castle. But the dwarfs had arrived.

"There she goes!" cried Doc. "After her!" The men chased her up a rocky hill and out onto a cliff, overhanging a deep ravine.

As the dwarfs came closer, the frightened Queen clambered further out onto the rocky ledge. Panic gripped her as she realised that she was trapped.

In desperation, the Queen began to loosen an enormous boulder and push it towards the dwarfs. "I'll fix you!" she screamed. "I'll crush your bones!"

But just as the boulder started to come free, a bolt of lightning hit the rock. The ledge shattered and fell, taking the boulder and the wicked Queen with it. There was a blood-curdling howl as the Queen plunged to her death on the rocks below.

The dwarfs hurried back to their cottage, only to find Snow White lying pale and still on the floor. "She – she's dead," stammered Sleepy.

She looked so beautiful and as if she were only sleeping. The little men could not bear to bury her, so they made a crystal coffin and carried it to the forest. There the lovely Princess lay, surrounded by flowers, and the dwarfs kept watch beside her day and night.

One day a handsome young man came riding through the forest. He was the very same Prince who had met Snow White by the well. When he saw her lying in the coffin, he got down from his horse and came to gaze at her. He bent over her still body and kissed her tenderly.

All at once Snow White's eyes opened. She was alive! When she saw the Prince, her face lit up with joy. As the dwarfs cheered and danced with happiness, the Prince took Snow White in his arms.

"Goodbye, my dear friends," Snow White said to the dwarfs. "I shall never forget you." She kissed each one of them on the forehead.

The Prince lifted Snow White onto his horse. "Goodbye, Princess!" the dwarfs called, as the pair rode out of sight. They would miss their beloved Snow White, but they were glad that she had found her true love at last.

Snow White and her prince – and the seven dwarfs – lived happily ever after.